LATINOS IN BASEBALL

Moises Alou

An Authorized Biography

Carrie Muskat

Mitchell Lane Publishers, Inc.
P.O. Box 200
Childs, MD 21916-0200

LATINOS IN BASEBALL

Tino Martinez	Bobby Bonilla	Roberto Alomar	Pedro Martinez
Moises Alou	Sammy Sosa	Ivan Rodriguez	Carlos Baerga
Ramon Martinez	Alex Rodriguez	Vinny Castilla	Mariano Rivera

Library of Congress Cataloging-in-Publication Data

Muskat, Carrie
    Moises Alou / Carrie Muskat.
      p. cm. — (Latinos in baseball)
    Includes index.
    Summary: Presents a biography of the son of baseball great Felipe Alou, who grew up to lead the Florida Marlins to victory in the 1997 World Series.
    ISBN 1-883845-86-6 (lib. bdg.)
    1. Alou, Moises, 1966- —Juvenile literature. 2. Baseball players—United States—Juvenile literature. [1. Alou, Moises, 1966- . 2. Baseball players. 3. Latin Americans—Biography.]
I. Title. II. Series.
GV865.A39M87 1999
796.357' 092—dc21
[B]
                                              98-48046
                                              CIP
                                              AC

About the Author: Carrie Muskat has covered major league baseball since 1981, beginning with United Press International in Minneapolis. She was UPI's lead writer at the 1991 World Series. A freelance journalist since 1992, she is a regular contributor to *USA Today* and *USA Today Baseball Weekly*. Her work has appeared in the *Chicago Tribune*, *Inside Sports*, and *ESPN Total Sports* magazine. She is the author of several baseball books for children, including *Barry Bonds* (Chelsea House), *Sammy Sosa* (Mitchell Lane), and *Mark McQwire* (Chelsea House).

Photo Credits: cover photo: Jose L. Marin/Marin and Associates; p. 4 Reuters/Marc Serota/Archive Photos; pp. 12, 49, 50, 53 © 1998 Florida Marlins/Denis Bancroft; p. 21 UPI/Corbis-Bettmann; p. 35 AP Photo; p. 43 Reuters/Jeff Christensen/Archive Photos; pp. 56, 58, 61, 62 © 1998 Houston Astros.

Acknowledgments: The following story was developed based on the author's personal interviews with Moises Alou during the 1998 baseball season. Professional and personal friends and family members were also interviewed for this book, including Felipe Alou. The final version was approved for print by Moises Alou. This story has been thoroughly researched and checked for accuracy. To the best of our knowledge, it represents a true story.

Mitchell Lane PUBLISHERS

TABLE OF CONTENTS

Moises Alou raises his arm in the air as he runs down the first baseline after hitting a three-run home run in the fourth inning of game one of the World Series against the Cleveland Indians, October 18, 1997.

CHAPTER ONE
The World Series

The state of Florida has been host to major-league spring training camps since the early 1900s. The Pittsburgh Pirates were the first team to locate there, calling St. Petersburg, Florida, its spring home in 1911. By the 1920s, the New York Yankees and Atlanta Braves had set up camps in Florida. When the regular season started, the teams broke camp and headed north. Florida baseball fans were left with no team to call their own. Today, 20 teams have training camps in the Sunshine State, and Florida has two major-league teams—the Florida Marlins and the Tampa Bay Devil Rays.

In 1991, Major League Baseball awarded the city of Miami an expansion team. Floridians were thrilled with the news. On April 5, 1993, the Florida Marlins played their first game and beat the Los Angeles Dodgers 6-3 before a sellout crowd of 42,334.

Expansion teams usually need time to develop their players, and the Marlins were not expected to do well in the beginning. In their first year, the team finished 64-98, good for sixth place in the National League East. The Marlins improved each successive season and went 80-82 in 1996 to finish third in the East.

Marlins owner Wayne Huizenga wanted to speed up the process and do better. He gave general manager Dave Dombrowski the go-ahead to spend money on talented free-agent players to make the young team a contender. One of the first things Dombrowski did was hire veteran Jim Leyland as the Marlins manager in October 1996. Leyland had been to the postseason three times as a manager with the Pittsburgh Pirates but had never won the World Series.

The Marlins already had outfielders Gary Sheffield and Devon White and pitchers Kevin Brown and Robb Nen on the roster. In November 1996, the team signed third baseman Bobby Bonilla. In early December, they added young pitcher Alex Fernandez and versatile utilityman Jim Eisenreich.

On December 12, 1996, the Marlins completed their free-agent acquisitions by adding outfielder Moises Alou. Little did they know they had just acquired their most valuable player.

"The team we're going to have right now, there's no way we're not going to make it to the playoffs," Alou said at the time. How right he was.

Alou had played for the Montreal Expos since 1990. In 1996, the slender outfielder was coming off one of his best seasons. He had played in a career-high 143 games in Montreal and established personal highs in at-bats, runs scored, hits, and, the most important category to a team, runs batted in (RBIs).

The Expos were a small-market team and had to keep a low payroll. Moises knew the team could not afford to pay him the same as what other six-year players who had his kind of offensive numbers were getting.

There was a catch, however. Moises' father, Felipe, was the Expos manager. Being together with their fathers is something very few athletes have a chance to do. "Go where they show you the money," Felipe told his son. The business of baseball made Moises' decision easier.

So, Moises signed a five-year, $25 million contract with the Marlins. His $5 million per year was a small but significant part of the $89 million Wayne Huizenga spent in building the 1997 Florida Marlins.

The Marlins were the perfect team for Alou. Miami, where the team was based, was close to his home, the Dominican Republic. He liked the strong Hispanic population in the area. He felt comfortable there and it showed on the field. He was named an All-Star for the second time in his career and set career highs in six offensive categories, including home runs (23) and RBIs (115).

The team pieced together by Dombrowski gelled. Leyland guided the high-priced Marlins to a 92-70 record and second place in the National League East behind Atlanta. Florida had the fourth best record in the National League and qualified for the playoffs as a wild card team.

The Marlins' first postseason opponent was the West division champion San Francisco Giants in a best-of-five series. Alou contributed some big hits. In Game 2, he hit the game-winning RBI single in the bottom of the ninth for a 7-6 Marlins victory. In Game 3, he connected on a two-out single in the top of the sixth, doubled and scored on White's grand slam as the Marlins won 6-2. The Marlins swept the series, winning three straight games.

Pitching-rich Atlanta was next. The Marlins had beaten the Braves in eight of 12 games played between the two teams during the regular season, but Florida was still an underdog going into the National League Championship Series (NLCS). Alou helped get the best-of-seven series started in Game 1 on October 7 with a three-run double in the top of the fourth inning. He added a fourth RBI in the Marlins' 5-3 win.

His defensive efforts in Game 1 nearly cost him. Alou hurt his wrist when he banged his arm on the top of the outfield fence going after Ryan Klesko's sixth-inning home run. Alou also strained his right hamstring on the play. Funny thing was, the hamstring was the only thing sore when he left the ballpark.

"I guess it was the excitement of the game," he said. "I iced my hamstring, but my wrist didn't feel hurt."

But when Alou woke up the next day and tried to push himself out of bed, he fell. He couldn't grip a bat, either, and did not play in Game 2 on October 8, which the Marlins lost 7-1 to even the series, 1-1.

Alou did not suffer any significant damage to his wrist and received a cortisone shot to dull the pain. He missed the team practice on the off day, October 9, but he had a good excuse. Alou was with his wife, Austria, who delivered the couple's third child, Kirby Thomas Alou, on that day. The child is named after former Minnesota Twins outfielder Kirby Puckett. The birth was induced a few weeks early so that Moises could be present and so that Austria could attend the World Series games, if there were any.

"Now, when my team needs me the most, I get hurt," Moises said during an interview from the hospital. "I feel terrible about that. But this is a great, great day. Look how happy I am. Can't you see it on my face?"

The Marlins pitchers had their game faces on when they upstaged the Braves during the NLCS. Rookie Livan Hernandez struck out 15 batters in Game 5 in front of a cheering crowd of 51,982 at Pro Player Stadium in Miami. Ace Kevin Brown, battling a stomach ailment, then pitched a complete game in Game 6 to send Florida into the World Series.

Alou had struggled along with his teammates against Atlanta. The Marlins hit just .199 against the Braves pitchers, and Alou had one hit in 15 at-bats. After the four-RBI opener, he had driven in only one more run.

The World Series was next. The Marlins, the surprise National League champions, would face the American League champions, the Cleveland Indians.

"I'll be nervous because I've never played in a World Series," Alou admitted, "but I won't be scared. It's like Opening Day . . . only more meaningful."

If the World Series were going to be anything like Opening Day, Alou would do great. He had hit a home run in the Marlins' opener against the Chicago Cubs on April 1 in a 4-2 win.

It was a hot, humid night on October 18 for Game 1 of the World Series. With 67,245 fans packed into Pro Player Stadium and the game tied 1-1 in the fourth inning, Alou connected on a good pitch, down and away, and hit a three-run homer off Cleveland pitcher Orel Hershiser. The ball hit the left-field foul pole. Charles Johnson also homered as Florida won 7-4.

Cleveland won Game 2 by a 6-1 score behind strong pitching from Chad Ogea. Alou had two doubles in the game. The scene then shifted to Jacobs Field in Cleveland for Games 3, 4, and 5. Used to hot and humid weather, the players wore knit caps and long underwear to counter the cold. Game 3 was a sloppy affair as both teams committed three errors each and numerous other blunders in the Marlins' 14-11 win.

Marlins bench coach Jerry Manuel gave Alou a little pep talk before Game 4. He told Alou that he needed to be more of "a hitter, not a swinger." Alou responded. In Game 4, the wind chill reading at game time was a bitter 15 degrees, the coldest World Series game ever played. The Indians must have had more long underwear than the warm-weather Marlins: they won 10-3. Alou hit his second homer of the series in that game.

In Game 5 on October 23, Alou brought the Marlins back from a 4-2 deficit with another three-run homer, a 400-foot blast, again off Hershiser. Hershiser had tried to fool Alou, a fastball hitter, with a steady diet of junk pitches. The veteran right-hander had made Alou look bad his first two trips to the plate. In the sixth inning, Alou fouled a slider back. Hershiser then hung another slider and Alou made contact, launching the ball over the center-field wall.

"He hit it 580 feet," Indians manager Mike Hargrove said, describing Alou's homer. "He crushed it."

After 14 postseason games, Alou had 15 RBIs. "I was still driving guys in and that's what I count on," Alou said.

"He's gotten a lot of big, big hits for us," Leyland said.

Alou's blast opened a 6-4 lead, and he added a single in the eighth and an RBI single in the ninth in the Marlins' 8-7 win.

The series shifted back to warm Florida. Ogea again stifled the Marlins in Game 6, and the Indians won 4-1 before 67,498 people to tie the series 3-3.

The world championship of the 1997 baseball season was to be settled in one game, Game 7.

Before the Marlins took the field, Leyland gathered the players in the clubhouse. "Next time we're in this room," he told the team, "we'll be world champions."

Sheffield led the players in prayer and dedicated the game to Leyland. Al Leiter started for the Marlins against Cleveland's young sensation Jaret Wright. Tony Fernandez gave the Indians a 2-0 lead with a two-run single in the third inning. Bonilla closed the gap to 2-1 with a leadoff home run in the seventh.

The Marlins were down by one run in the bottom of the ninth and three outs away from losing the championship. Alou, who had come through in the clutch all season, singled to lead off, looping the ball to center off Cleveland's Jose Mesa. Bonilla then struck out. Johnson singled and Alou advanced to third.

"I was thinking about a celebration, the trophy, friends, a lot of things," Cleveland shortstop Omar Vizquel said.

The Indians were two outs away.

Craig Counsell, who three months earlier was playing in Triple A, then lined a ball to right, which Cleveland's Manny Ramirez caught at the warning track. Alou scored on the sacrifice fly and the game was tied 2-2.

For only the third time in World Series history, Game 7 went into extra innings. The Marlins loaded the bases with two outs in the 11th, and Edgar Renteria came through with a single up the middle to score Counsell from third. It was the 29th time in 1997 that the Marlins had won a game in the last at-bat, and it came in the team's biggest game of its young history.

The crowd of 67,204 exploded in cheers. Not only were the Marlins the first wild card entry to qualify for the postseason, but they won a World Championship faster than any expansion team in history. Florida had had to rally, coming from behind in eight of their 11 postseason wins.

"That was an unbelievable feeling. The World Series was unbelievable," Alou said.

Cuban refugee Livan Hernandez was named Most Valuable Player for the Series, but many felt Alou was more

LATINOS IN BASEBALL

Moises displays the 1997 World Series trophy. It was the first such honor for the Florida Marlins and for Moises Alou.

deserving. Hernandez was a great story hyped by the national media covering the Series. Just 22 years old in October 1997, Hernandez had played two years with the Cuban National team. He defected on September 27, 1995, while in Monterrey, Mexico, leaving his country and his family behind. Hernandez had been training for the 1995 World Cup when he defected. The Cup event was to be played later that year in Havana. Hernandez had signed with the Marlins as a free agent in January 1996, and his sad life story plus sudden success in the World Series got lots of attention.

"I looked at this as the best team effort in the postseason that I've ever seen," Bonilla said. "I don't think one player asked could say who was the MVP. Everybody had something to do with us winning the games."

While the spotlight focused on rookie pitcher Hernandez in his two starts, Alou had simply picked up where he left off at the end of the regular season when he led Florida with 115 RBIs. He was locked in against the Indians, finishing with a .321 average. Alou had nine hits, including three home runs and two doubles, and drove in nine runs.

"I didn't think that we were playing the World Series or that there were 200 million people watching or 70,000 [fans at] every game in Florida and 50,000 in Cleveland," Alou said. "I was just playing. It was like playing a regular game."

Actually, Alou was so focused on the game and his mission that he didn't realize how many people were packed into Pro Player Stadium or Jacobs Field until he saw photos in magazines and newspapers after the Series ended.

There was one face missing among the 400,000 who attended the seven World Series games. About 25 of Alou's family had flown to Miami from the Dominican Republic to watch Moises play in the Series. Alou's father, Felipe, was not among them. He had to put his love of his son aside because of his loyalty to the Montreal Expos. Felipe Alou felt it would be wrong for him as the manager of a rival team to be shown cheering for another team, even if he was only rooting for his son.

"I'm with the Montreal Expos," Felipe said, trying to explain. "I managed against the Florida Marlins. I'm not your average Joe Fan. I'm a major-league manager. When I'm out of this job and Moises or one of my other sons is in a World Series, I will be the first man to be there. But if I am a major-league manager, I don't believe it looks right to be on camera talking to people.

"I was dying every time he came up to the plate and hoping he could do well," said Felipe, who did watch the Series on television. "But there was no way Felipe Alou could go to the World Series [and cheer for the Marlins] and two days later receive a check from the Montreal Expos. I can't do that." Moises understood.

"I agreed with his decision," Moises said. "I called him a couple times whenever I had a good game. I called him to share it with him. I called before Game 6 and he said, 'Are you guys going to do it tonight?' and I said I thought so."

Felipe Alou had a more personal reason to skip the Series. He had undergone surgery after the season ended and needed some time at home to recuperate and fish, one of his favorite hobbies—besides watching his son play baseball. Moises knew his dad was pulling for him.

"I don't know how they could not give Moises the MVP of the Series," Manuel said. "I could understand the sympathy for Livan, but when you look back at the num-

bers, Moises rose and that's what his father would've wanted, which was for him to be the best when it was time to be the best."

Hershiser, off whom Moises hit two home runs in the Series, also cast his vote for the Marlins left fielder.

"He was the MVP," Hershiser said of his young nemesis. "Livan pitched great, but Moises playing every day and hitting the way he did and hitting the two three-run homers off me really put them over the top. If you look at when he hit those home runs and when they came in the Series, they were turning points."

Father and son are together whenever they can manage it. Unfortunately, Felipe (right) could not be present at the 1997 World Series because it would have been viewed as a conflict of interest. Felipe manages the Montreal Expos. But earlier in the year, at spring training, Felipe and Moises were reunited, wearing different uniforms for the first time in five years.

Moises did not get a chance to hit any more home runs for the Marlins. On November 11, just 16 days after winning the world championship, Alou was traded to the Houston Astros. It was the first step in the Marlins' massive cost-cutting scheme.

In early April 1998, Alou received the coveted World Series ring during a presentation by Dombrowski. The Astros, Alou's new team, were playing the Giants, and Dombrowski gave Alou his ring outside the visitors' clubhouse at 3Com Park in San Francisco.

"The players that contributed, we wanted to make sure to get it to them as soon as we could afterwards because they deserve it," Dombrowski said. "It's not their fault they are not there at that time."

"I kind of had mixed feelings about getting my ring," Alou said. "My dad never got one, and a bunch of good players never got one. I feel, why me? I've got to be thankful and thank the Lord every day. It wasn't easy. It has been a long road for me. Now, I finally have it in hand."

Valued at an estimated $6,000 to $8,000, each Marlins ring features diamonds in a platinum-and-14-karat-gold setting. The Marlins' logo is on top, and one side is inscripted with the player's name, position, and number, along with sunshine rays and waves representing South Florida. The other side has a picture of the World Series trophy and the words *One heartbeat*, the motto Leyland coined in his original talk when he joined the Marlins in 1997. Inside, Alou's name and *1997 National League All-Star* are imprinted.

Alou had made the most out of his only season with the Marlins. And he had a World Championship ring.

"This," Alou said of the ring, "is what it's all about."

CHAPTER 2
In the Beginning

Baseball was a daily ritual in the Dominican Republic for Felipe, Mateo, and Jesus Alou when they were growing up in the town of Haina. Sometimes they used small coconuts as a ball. The coconuts didn't last long. None of the brothers had a glove, but they improvised, stitching together scraps of canvas with fishing line. They turned branches into bats.

The boys' father, Jose, was a hard-working carpenter who didn't want his sons to play baseball. Baseball, he said, was for idle people. But in the Dominican Republic, baseball was part of the children's lives. Felipe and his brothers and friends were so intent on playing, they cut down trees to make room for a field. They got caught, but the family started to realize how serious the trio was about the game.

Felipe's uncle gave him his first glove, a Wilson model, and told the boy to put oil on it to soften it. Felipe used cooking oil, which was not what his uncle meant. The next day, he discovered rats had eaten holes in the glove. Felipe once got a pair of baseball shoes with spikes, but one day his father needed shoes for work and took off the spikes so that he could wear them.

"Back in the Dominican Republic, there were what we called 'rules of the hour,'" Felipe said. "Sometimes if you were too good a hitter, the other team would say, 'If you put him in the lineup, we're not playing.' So, the guy would have to sit out and watch. There were many times I did not play."

Felipe was good enough to compete on the Dominican national team that beat the U.S. team for the gold medal in the 1954 Pan-Am Games. Jose and Virginia, Felipe's mother, wanted their son to be a doctor, not a ballplayer. In 1955, the 20-year-old Felipe was studying medicine at the University of Santo Domingo in the Dominican Republic.

"I was studying to be a doctor," Felipe said. "I didn't say I wanted to be a doctor."

Horacio Martinez was the athletic director at the university and also was scouting for the New York Giants baseball team. He had watched Felipe play and offered him a major-league contract for 200 pesos, which was about $200. Felipe agreed.

"That may not sound like much," Felipe said, "but it helped pay the man who used to sell us food on credit."

And his parents?

"They were very disappointed," Felipe said. "They didn't want me to be a player."

In the 1950s, baseball was a major local sport in the Dominican Republic. Players from the Dominican Republic had competed in the Negro League, the Cuban League, and the Puerto Rican League, but at that time no one from the island had played in the U.S. major leagues. Baseball was not a "profession" at that time, but not because there weren't any talented players.

"There was a perception at that time that the Latin players weren't intelligent. All we did was eat rice and beans and plantains," Felipe said. "I looked around when that opportunity came and I know the last thing Mr. Martinez wanted to do was take me out of school. He also knew my family, and the truth was this: we were in trouble and I was the oldest child in a family of six. My dad was not making enough money to get me through college. I was really draining the family finances by going to school. I was getting some help from an uncle who was in the Dominican army.

"So I said, I think I'll give this baseball a shot," Felipe said. "I had played the year before against the Americans in the Pan-Am Games. I was the cleanup hitter, and I did very well against the Americans in the two games we played them. I said to myself, 'These are the best college players in the United States and we beat them big time.' I told my family I wanted to give this a shot and if it doesn't work, then maybe we can find a way for me to go back to college."

The Giants assigned Felipe Alou to their minorleague team in Lake Charles, Louisiana, of the Evangeline League. The 1950s were a difficult time for a black man in the United States. There were racial tensions, and some of the towns in the league had a rule prohibiting black athletes and white athletes from competing on the same field. "Half the games I traveled to, I had to sit in the bleachers with the black fans," Felipe said. "Some places, like Baton Rouge, they didn't even let me in the stadium. It was hard to swallow, but I knew what I was getting into before I came. I couldn't speak English. But I was no fool. I had my goals set on baseball. Nothing was going to disrupt me."

The only word of English that Felipe knew was *yes*. The problem was, nobody said yes. Everyone said yeah.

"I had to ask a person what *yeah* means and he said *yeah* means 'yes,'" Felipe said. "I said, 'Welcome to the U.S.A.'"

After one month, the Giants switched Felipe to Cocoa in the Florida State League. He had started to understand some English and was able to go to the grocery store and buy cake and milk for a snack. Felipe didn't make much money, but what he did make, he sent home to his family in the Dominican Republic.

Felipe was a natural player. He had never had any formal baseball training. One player in Florida told him, "You hit ugly." It didn't matter to Felipe what they said. He could hit and he knew it. He proved it, leading the Florida State League with a .380 average in 1956. And he survived.

The black and Latin players would stay in separate hotels from the white players, although the places didn't look like hotels. In Gainesville, Florida, they lived on the second floor of a building. The floor was made of wood, and it was so rough and weak, they had to walk softly so that the boards would not give way.

The Cocoa team didn't have a bus. They used three station wagons to travel to away games. Felipe's teammates included two Puerto Ricans, Julio Navarro and Hector Cruz, a black player named Chuck Howard, and Miami native Jim Miller. "I'll never forget them," Felipe said. "They were my friends. The white players were my friends, too, but they were only my friends at the ballpark. I didn't see the whites in the city. I only saw them at the ballpark."

Nothing in Felipe's upbringing had prepared him for the prejudice he experienced in the U.S. His father was a black Dominican, the son of a slave. His mother came from a Spanish family.

"The players today don't know how tough it was. I'm glad they don't," Felipe said. "Many times, the dignity of a man was put to the test, especially because I was a college student and not only that, I was a good college student. I didn't know anything about race when I got there. To me, it didn't make any difference. But when I got here, I had to eat away from the rest of the team. It was like hiding."

The one thing he could count on was baseball. Felipe was called up to the Giants, who were then in San Francisco, in 1958. He was the second Dominican to reach the majors. Ozzie Virgil had been the first, making his debut on September 23, 1956, with New York.

Felipe played six solid seasons with San Francisco, including all seven games of the 1962 World Series. On September 15, 1963, he and his brothers made history by playing in the same outfield for the Giants against the New York Mets.

"As it happened, we didn't think it was anything special, but we look back now and say, 'Wait a minute! Three brothers in the same major-league outfield at the same time? That's never happened before or after,'" Felipe said.

The San Francisco Giants became the first major league team to use three brothers in the same game when Jesus, 21, (left), Matty, 24, (center), and Felipe Alou, 29, (right), all batted in the eighth inning against the New York Mets in September 1963. Unfortunately, all three brothers made outs and the Mets won the game, 4–2.

Felipe was traded to the Milwaukee Braves in December 1963 in a seven-player deal. He kept on hitting, and in 1966 he led the National League in hits (218), runs (122), total bases (355), and at-bats (666), and finished second to his brother Matty in the race for the batting championship.

That same year—1966—Felipe and his wife, Maria Beltre, celebrated the birth of their third son, Moises, on July 3 in Atlanta, Georgia.

Felipe, Matty, and Jesus Alou made quite an impression in the major leagues. Felipe had the most extra-base power, hitting 20 homers and 30 doubles four times each. A three-time all-star, Felipe retired in 1974 with a career average .286. Matty, the middle brother, won the National League batting title in 1966 while a member of the Pittsburgh Pirates with a .342 average—111 points higher than his previous season. A left-handed hitter, Matty reached the .330 mark in three other seasons and finished his 15-year big-league career with a .307 average. Jesus averaged .280 over 15 big-league seasons, and his most notable game was July 10, 1964, when he collected six hits off an equal number of Chicago pitchers. Jesus, then a member of the Giants, singled off Dick Ellsworth, Lew Burdette, Don Elston, Wayne Schurr, and Lindy McDaniel and homered off Dick Scott.

When Jesus notched his 1,000th hit, it not only made the Alous the only triumvirate of brothers to reach that mark but also assured them of first place in combined career hits for three or more siblings. The three DiMaggio brothers totaled 4,853 hits. The three Alous combined for 5,094.

The Alou family name was well respected by baseball people. Young Moises heard about his father's and uncles' heroics from his older brothers, Felipe Jr. and Jose. When Moises was two years old, Felipe divorced the boys' mother, Maria, but he stayed close to the family. Felipe made sure the family had a nice house in a nice neighborhood in Santo Domingo, the capital of the Dominican Republic.

"I have divorced," Felipe said, "but I have never divorced my children. I've always been very close to my children, every one of them."

Moises had to grow up quickly.

"It's something that made me a tougher kid than the rest of the kids," Moises said. "Growing up in my neighborhood, everybody lived with their mom and dad and had their dad to spoil them and guard them and take care of them. I didn't have that. I was pretty much on my own. I've got to give my mom all the credit in the world for the way she brought me and my brothers up."

Tragedy struck the Alou family on March 26, 1976. Felipe, who was in spring training as a coach for the Montreal Expos, received a phone call that day from Maria. Their oldest son, 16-year-old Felipe Jr., had died in a swimming pool accident. Jose and Moises were 12 and nine years old, respectively, at that time.

Felipe immediately returned home to the Dominican Republic to deal with his grief.

"The pain of losing a child stays with you forever," Felipe said. "For almost a year, I really wanted to do nothing, nothing at all."

Felipe Jr. had been more than a big brother to Moises.

"He was almost like a father to me," Moises said. "He was only 16, but he acted 25. He would never let me leave the table until I had finished all my food. He was the one who really taught me how to play. I was seven years younger than he was, but I went everywhere with him. For me, growing up, he was the man of the house."

Sports became an outlet for Moises. Every day, kids in his Santo Domingo neighborhood would play a game called *la vitilla*. They would take a broomstick and cut it to the length of a baseball bat. The ball was actually a bottle cap from a gallon-sized water or milk bottle. The pitcher would spin the tiny cap to the hitter, who had to try to make contact. To make an out, you had to catch the cap before it stopped moving. *Vitilla* comes from *vista*, which means "sight."

"*Vitilla* is supposed to give you good sight to play baseball," Moises said. "The cap is like a boomerang or a Frisbee, and to hit it with a broomstick is pretty hard.

"Believe it or not, I was a better left-handed hitter playing *vitilla* than I was right-handed," said Moises, who swings right-handed now. "I never switch-hit in my life."

When the kids got tired of that game, they played another called *la plaquita*, which means "license plate." The children would take two license plates and fold the ends so that they stood up like soccer goals, then they would set them up at either end of a stretch of street. The game was similar to field hockey as teams of two players each tried to hit the license plates.

"There weren't many fields in the Dominican Republic," Moises said. "A lot of people play on the streets and we make up games."

At this time, other Dominicans had made it to the major leagues. The kids had heard about George Bell, Pedro Guerrero, Tony Pena, and Joaquin Andujar. Many children skipped school to try to make it to the big leagues. The lure of quick money attracted them. Moises attended Centro Especializado de Ensenanza, a high school in Santo

Domingo, but he did not play baseball there because the school did not have a team. He found another sport—basketball.

"I was the tallest guy on my team and I was a guard, a point guard," he said. "When I went to junior college, I didn't play basketball for a year and I came back and tried to play and I lost it. I never got the touch back."

His parents tried to develop Moises' and his brother Jose's baseball talent in the exclusive Manny Mota baseball school, run by the former major-league outfielder who had played 20 seasons, primarily with the Los Angeles Dodgers.

"I knew Moises had talent because of his great arm and the way he could run and his build," Felipe said. "It's not so much being my son but being a Dominican. Baseball runs through the blood of the Dominican kids. You find that with everybody."

Moises joined Mota's league when he was seven years old and played off and on for about seven years.

"He was a good basketball player, but somehow we convinced him to play baseball and join the Little League," Mota said. "He showed some tools and ability when he first joined us. He was one of the best players. You could see the talent. He looked like his father the first time we saw him play."

Moises had baseball in his blood. He also had a strong commitment to his mother. He would play in the Manny Mota league for three or four Saturdays in a row, then stop for about a month.

"I liked playing basketball better," Moises said. "Sometimes on a Saturday, I had to help my mom out at home and clean. So, some Saturdays, even if I wanted to go, I couldn't." How many kids can relate to that?

CHAPTER 3
Early Years in Baseball

Being from a famous baseball family could have been difficult for Moises because of the expectations placed on him. His father and uncles had done so well in the major leagues, Moises might have felt some pressure to do even better.

"The kids, his teammates, they looked up to him because they knew he was Felipe Alou's son," said Manny Mota. "He didn't get any special treatment because of it. He was an example for the rest of the kids in the league. He always worked harder than the other kids and he was a very disciplined boy. He was always on time, had good manners, and always showed respect."

Moises wasn't sure he wanted to follow in his father's footsteps.

"When I was in high school, I had no clue about what I wanted to be," Moises said. "I don't know if I wanted to be a baseball player. I wanted to go to school."

With help from Mota and others, Moises was able to get a scholarship to attend Canada (pronounced Can-YA-da) College in Redwood City, California. It was a junior college, and Moises wanted to post good grades so that he could attend a four-year school. His father gave him $500 as a going-away present, and Moises put that money in a bank, hoping to save up enough someday for tuition for a four-year school.

Moises had no trouble adjusting to baseball in the United States. He led the team in batting his freshman year with a .340 average.

After his first year, Moises took summer-school classes at Marin College in Indiana, studying theology and psychology. It was no coincidence that his father was managing the Expos' Triple-A team in Indianapolis. For the first time that he could remember, Moises was able to spend a lot of time with his father.

"Whenever the Indians were in town, I went to their games and practiced with my dad," Moises said. "In the daytime I would go to school, and at night I spent time with my dad. He would take me back to the dorms every night. I had a good time there and I played in the summer league, which helped a lot."

Moises had spent many days playing *la vitilla* in the streets, but he had not played much organized baseball. This was a chance to smooth the rough edges.

"When I went back to junior college [at Canada], I was way ahead of everybody," Moises said. "The two months I was there in Indiana, I learned so much, working out with my dad every day, taking infield. I had a better arm than everybody on the [Indianapolis] team, and they were already professional players."

In his second season at Canada, Moises hit .474. He led the conference in batting but still wasn't thinking about becoming a professional ballplayer. It wasn't until January 14, 1986, that he thought about turning pro. On that day, Moises was the second player taken in the amateur draft, selected by the Pittsburgh Pirates.

"I still wasn't sure I was going to sign," Moises said. "I had this friend of mine at school and her mom told me, 'I think you should sign because you're probably going to have an opportunity to play baseball once in your life. School will always be there.' That meant a lot to me."

Moises called his father to tell him he was going to sign with the Pirates. The team was offering Moises a $75,000 signing bonus. Times had changed from when Felipe had signed in the 1950s and was paid about $200.

"My father had told my brother Jose that he didn't want my brother to sign when he was drafted in the second round by the Expos," Moises said. "He wanted my brother to go back to school. He did go back to school in Florida and didn't do that good. So I signed, and that was it."

Moises finished his school year before signing with the Pirates on May 23, 1986. He was assigned to the Pirates' Class-A team Watertown in the New York–Penn League and made a splash. His first pro home run was a grand slam June 24 against Jamestown. He led the league in triples with eight and batted .236.

He missed part of the 1987 minor-league season because of an injured shoulder, and in 1988 he batted .313 for Augusta. Moises kept moving up through the Pirates' minor-league system, playing for Salem and then Harrisburg in 1989. That was a significant year personally for the young outfielder. On May 15, 1989, he married his childhood sweetheart, Austria. They had met in a very strange way in 1983.

"The school year had just started and she was new in school," Moises said. "I saw her a couple times and liked her right away. I was fighting with a friend of mine, just joking and kicking each other, and I accidently hit her and kicked her in the back. I said, 'I'm so sorry.' The next day, I asked her if she was OK. So that's how we met."

Married life seemed to agree with Moises. He batted .302 with 14 home runs at Salem in 1989 and was promoted to Harrisburg, where he hit .293.

The next season was a busy one. Moises changed uniforms five times, playing for three minor-league teams and two major-league teams. He started the 1990 season at Class AA Harrisburg and was called up to the Pirates' major-league team on July 26. Less than 24 hours later, his cousin, Mel Rojas, a pitcher, was called up to the Phillies to make his major-league debut that night. It is the only time in major-league history that cousins have been called up for their major-league debuts on the same day.

Moises remembers his first game on July 26. He had arrived just before the game started and the Pirates were being shut out, losing by seven or eight runs. Veteran outfielder Andy Van Slyke sought out Alou on the bench.

"Hey, Mo, we're not that bad," Van Slyke said jokingly.

"I knew I was going to get in the game, so I started getting a little nervous," Moises said. "I remember eating sunflower seeds and my hands started getting sweaty. All of a sudden in the sixth inning, I'm in the game. I played defense, left field, and I was nervous. They hit a ball to me right away. I got it and after that I was fine. Even when I went to hit, I was fine. I was comfortable."

He also was a little eager.

"I swung at the first pitch of my first at-bat, and I swung at the first pitch my second at-bat," Moises said. "I swung at the first pitch because I wanted to get the first hit out of the way. Ever since then, I've been swinging at the first pitch all the time. I think I got into a bad habit."

Van Slyke, a popular player with the Pirates, joked with Alou to get him to relax.

"When somebody comes up for their first game and they say they're not nervous, they're lying," Moises said.

Moises got his first major-league hit on July 28, a single off Philadelphia's Bruce Ruffin, but his major-league experience was short-lived. The Pirates already had a talented outfield at that time with Barry Bonds in left, Van Slyke in center, and Bobby Bonilla in right. Moises was sent back to the minors, to Triple-A Buffalo on July 29.

Pittsburgh needed a pitcher for the stretch run and made a deal with the Montreal Expos. On August 8, the Pirates acquired left-hander Zane Smith and sent left-handed pitcher Scott Ruskin and infielder Willie Greene, plus a player to be named later, to the Expos. Alou was that fourth player. He was traded to the Expos August 16 and called up on September 1 when major-league teams were allowed to expand their 25-man rosters.

Moises wanted to make the Expos' big-league roster in 1991, so he spent the off-season playing for his father, who was managing Escogido in the Dominican Winter League. But in November 1990, Moises injured his right shoulder diving back into a base on a pickoff attempt. He reported to the Expos spring training camp that year worried about the injury.

"At the time it happened, I wasn't established in the big leagues," Moises said. "I didn't know if I was going to come back and get a chance to play and be in the big leagues again. I thought I was going to go back to Triple A. That was tough."

One day during spring training, Moises was so upset about his shoulder that he started throwing as hard as he could.

"Mo, what are you doing? Are you crazy?" Expos teammate Andres Galarraga said.

"I'm tired of this," said Moises, who was crying.

Dr. Frank Jobe, a Los Angeles–based orthopedic specialist, was one of the best sports doctors in the country. Moises went to see Jobe because the Expos team doctor wasn't able to find anything wrong with the shoulder. Moises knew something was wrong. Jobe found two tears, a superior labrum tear and a rotator cuff tear, in Moises' right shoulder. He would need surgery, and his season was over.

"I started crying," Moises said. "I'm not a crybaby, but I love the game so much [and] I was afraid I wouldn't play again."

Jobe knew the young outfielder was scared. The doctor took Alou to the Los Angeles Dodgers clubhouse to introduce him to another player who had undergone similar surgery, pitcher Orel Hershiser.

Hershiser was doing his shoulder exercises when Alou and Jobe walked in.

"He told me how hard it was but he said, 'You're going to be OK,' and then we both started crying," Alou said.

"Moises was the first one I talked to about it, and I knew exactly what he was going through," Hershiser said. "He was the first guy who Dr. Jobe brought to me to inspire to come back. It dug up a lot of emotions for me of what I had to go through and how sorry I was feeling for him to have to go through. I told him there were going to be a lot of dark days, a lot of days when you don't think it worked. I told him to just keep working because it will work, it will turn out."

The two probably never imagined they would meet again seven years later in a World Series. But playing in the Series was far from Alou's mind on April 10, 1991, when he underwent surgery. Moises did not play at all that year but devoted himself to rehabilitating his shoulder. He had no intentions of going back to the minor leagues. Moises reported to spring training in 1992 healthy and determined. He made the Expos' big-league team as the fourth outfielder.

That was a milestone year for father and son. At the start of the season, Felipe was a coach on Expos manager Tom Runnell's staff. On May 21, 1992, Moises and his father went fishing. Felipe had a secret that he wasn't ready to share with his son.

"We went fishing for northern pike," Moises said. "We left early because he said he had to meet with the general manager and he didn't say what for.

"The next day, I went to the ballpark and everybody is congratulating me and I said, 'What's going on?' They said, 'Your dad's the manager.'"

CHAPTER 4
Montreal

Felipe Alou had managed at every level in the minor leagues in the Montreal Expos system, finishing first three times and winning two championships—1981 at Class AAA Denver and 1991 at Class A West Palm. In 1990, Felipe was named manager of the year in the Florida State League, posting a 92-40 record, which was an all-time franchise high for wins. He also managed in the winter leagues for 12 seasons, winning the Caribbean World Series in 1990 at Escogido in the Dominican League.

In 1981 and '82, Alou's Triple-A teams won their divisions. The big-league Expos were struggling, and Felipe had to deal with constant questions about why he wasn't promoted as their manager. He was a coach on the Expos staff in 1984 and then manager Bill Virdon was fired, prompting more people to ask Felipe why he wasn't managing.

The only answer Felipe can give today is that the Expos weren't ready to hire a minority manager, especially a Latino.

"I don't think a lot of people felt comfortable about it, and I didn't feel comfortable," Felipe said. "It was hard on everybody, the minority thing. I wanted to go to A ball because I thought that over there, nobody would ever ask me anymore why they didn't give me the big-league job. That's what I did. I wanted to be put as far away as possible."

Baseball always has been slow to make changes. Frank Robinson was the first African-American to be named manager for a major-league team, getting the Cleveland Indians job in 1975. That was 28 years after the first

African-American player, Jackie Robinson, made his debut in Major League Baseball in 1947.

Felipe also remembered what he had had to go through in the minor leagues. "I am a veteran of prejudice," he said.

In 1992, Felipe was asked to be a bench coach with the Montreal Expos for manager Tom Runnells' staff. "I didn't want to do it," Felipe said. "I didn't want to go back to the big leagues and be a coach. I really was not born to be a coach. I knew that. I was the older one of the kids, and when I played ball, I was the cleanup guy. There was always a lot of responsibility on my shoulders. I was not supposed to be a coach."

The Expos respected Felipe's experience. They wanted him to be the bench coach because Runnells was young and Felipe knew a lot of the Expos players from his days in the minor leagues. It took nearly two months to convince Felipe to take the job. He finally agreed, but Runnells had a tough time. The Expos struggled to a 17-20 record and were in fourth place in the National League East when Runnells was fired in May. Felipe fought it, but he was promoted to manager. He didn't want the job because he felt Runnells should be given more time with the big-league club. The Expos management, however, decided to make the change.

On May 22, Felipe became the first Dominican-born manager in the major leagues. And he became the fifth person in major-league history to manage his son in a major-league game. The other manager-player, father-son combos are Connie and Earle Mack, Yogi and Dale Berra, Cal Ripken Sr. and Cal Ripken Jr., and Hal and Brian McRae.

"I was afraid for my dad," Moises said. "I was afraid of the team failing. I wasn't afraid my dad would fail. I knew my dad could manage. I knew that from the bottom of my

Expos manager Felipe Alou (right) gives some pointers to his son, Expos outfielder, Moises (left), March 1, 1996.

heart. We were playing so bad that I was afraid. I remember the first week or two, I wanted to do so good and win so bad. If we lost, I'd be mad all the time because I wanted my dad to do good."

The first day Felipe looked inside the manager's desk at Olympic Stadium used by Runnells, he found money collected for player fines. Felipe took the cash and issued refunds.

New manager, new start.

"He knows everything," Expos outfielder Cliff Floyd said. "He knows the weather. It's like he knows the outcome before it happens. If you can't play for him, you can't play for anybody."

On May 27, five days after Felipe took over the team, Moises hit his first major-league home run off Houston's Mark Portugal.

Managing his son was never a concern for Felipe. "I never thought it would be a problem," Felipe said. "I know I was a little harder on him than the other players because I knew he could take it. I knew my kid. He was a man. He was a man when he was two years old. I knew he could take the fact that I had to be a little harder on him and demand more than other people because I didn't want anyone to ever dream that there was special treatment. My kid was an everyday guy, not because the manager was his father but because he is an everyday guy in the big leagues."

At the beginning of Felipe's tenure as manager, father and son would go to dinner together. But that soon stopped. Baseball players don't usually go to dinner with their managers. Ballplayers hang out with other ballplayers.

"Both of us were very careful that other players or team officials wouldn't even dream that there was some favoritism," Felipe said. "I think we did it well."

Felipe did push Moises. "Sometimes I got mad at him, but now I appreciate that he treated me like that," Moises said. "He didn't want to show any favoritism with me. Sometimes he was a little too hard."

When the Expos were in St. Louis for a series, *Sporting News* asked Felipe and Moises to pose together for a photo to be used on the cover of the magazine. When Moises arrived at the ballpark that day, he saw that his name was not in the lineup. He refused to be photographed with his father.

"I [would get] into a little slump and he'd bench me for a day or two and I'd get mad," Moises said. "I saw players like Delino DeShields or Marquis Grissom or Larry Walker and if they got into a slump, they'd play every day. One day, I said, 'Why do you do that to me?' and he said, 'Those guys are making more money than you are. They have to play every day.' OK, then I understood.

"I appreciate everything he did for me," Moises said of his father. "Everything I know in this game, I owe to him."

The 1992 season was the first year father and son were together in the same place on Father's Day. The Expos were playing the Pirates that day in Pittsburgh. Moises slipped into the manager's office early and left a present on Felipe's desk.

Moises was the oldest member of the Expos outfield that year, joining center fielder Grissom and right fielder Walker. Because of his desire to make his father look good as the manager, he almost overdid it.

"We had to slow him down," Expos coach Jerry Manuel said of Moises. "We'd say, 'Mo, you don't have to kill yourself out there just because your dad is here.' He really went to another level of play."

If a ball was hit into the outfield anywhere remotely near Moises, he would do everything possible to get to it. When he got a hit, Moises would fly to first base like never before. He knew all about the struggles his father had gone through, how Felipe had persevered in the minor leagues. Moises wanted to make his father proud. "He had the mind-set and the heart of his father," Manuel said.

Felipe's presence improved the team. Montreal finished the year 87-75 and in second place, battling the Pittsburgh Pirates until the next-to-last weekend of the regular season.

"It was unbelievable. He took the job and turned the team around in two weeks," Moises said.

Although he had started the season as the fourth outfielder, Moises took over the starting left-field job from Ivan Calderon. In his first full year in the majors, Moises hit .282. He led all rookie players in batting, slugging, and on-base percentage, and finished second in the balloting for Rookie of the Year to Los Angeles Dodgers first baseman Eric Karros.

The next year, Moises earned his job as the Expos starting left fielder. He put together a 12-game hitting streak from April 27 to May 11 and hit .583 during the stretch. He stole a career-high 17 bases. His uncle Matty is the only Alou to steal as many as 17 in a season and he did so five times, including a family-high 23 in 1966 for the Pirates.

From July 6 to July 9, Moises tied an Expos record by hitting homers in four consecutive games. He drove in at least one run in eight consecutive games from July 5 to July 15. He hit .370 with six home runs and 11 RBIs during the week July 5-11 and earned National League Player of the Week honors.

It was a dream season. His father was comfortably in charge of the team, Moises was playing every day, and the Expos were challenging for a playoff berth.

On September 16, Montreal was playing in St. Louis in the last game of a series. Moises hit a ball and hustled around first base, trying to stretch his base hit into a double. Suddenly he stopped, and his left leg collapsed underneath him. He fell to the ground, writhing in pain.

"You could hear a pop, like plastic popping," said Manuel, who was coaching third base. "He just lay there. Luis Alicea went over to put the tag on him, but he had to walk away because he couldn't stand to see the way Moises' ankle looked."

"I heard the pop," Moises said. "Maybe it was so painful that I didn't feel the pain. It was so scary. I felt like I'd broken my leg in half. I've never seen anything like it. My toe was pointing backwards."

Alicea, the Cardinals second baseman, couldn't look. The second-base umpire had to turn away. St. Louis manager Joe Torre said he heard the pop from the dugout. Felipe Alou rushed from the Expos dugout to his son.

"My dad was right there and he looked strong," Moises said. "He said, 'C'mon, you're going to be all right.' I said, 'Dad, look at that mess.'"

Expos trainer Rod McClain was also among the first at Moises' side. "Am I going to play again?" Moises said.

"Sure, you're going to be all right," McClain said. "We'll fix it tonight."

Moises' mind was scrambling. He was having a great year and suddenly his foot was turned backward. He and Austria were thinking about buying their first house. It took about 45 minutes for the ambulance to get to the in-field to take Moises to a hospital. Would he play again?

"We left St. Louis without him because he had to have surgery," Manuel said. "We won the game, but the plane was really in mourning. His dad was very quiet. He's always quiet, but he was extra quiet at that time."

"They told me the plane was so quiet, it was like we'd lost the World Series," Moises said.

At the St. Louis hospital, the doctors diagnosed the injury. Moises had fractured his fibula and dislocated his left ankle. He was to have surgery in Montreal, so he flew back and called his father from the airport. Felipe said he wanted Moises to stop by the stadium to see his teammates, who were worried about the young outfielder. Moises went directly to Olympic Stadium from the airport.

"I called everybody together for a meeting and I started crying," Moises said, his eyes tearing up just remembering the day. "I told the guys I appreciated that they were worried about me and told them everything was going to be fine. I told them to keep playing hard. We were playing the Phillies that day and we were playing for the pennant. I was looking forward to that series—it was sold out in Montreal and I couldn't play. I was swinging the bat so good."

Surgery in Montreal was extensive. Two fixation screws were placed in the ankle to stabilize the joint. The foot and leg were placed in a cast, and the prognosis was good that the screws and cast would be removed in six weeks. Several of the Phillies players visited Moises in the hospital. He received thousands of get-well cards and even a fruit basket from Pirates manager Jim Leyland.

Alou was finished for the year. He had hit .286 with 18 home runs and 85 RBIs. But he wasn't finished playing.

CHAPTER 5
Comeback Player

S ix weeks after Moises Alou underwent surgery to repair his fractured ankle, he returned to Montreal to
have the cast and screws removed. His rehabilitation be-
gan in earnest in the winter of 1993. For at least six hours a
day, every day, he turned himself over to Expos assistant
trainer Mike Kozac. Moises would walk in the swimming
pool, undergo massage, and work on his balance. He returned to his home in the Dominican Republic and continued on his own, determined again to play baseball.

"That was my goal, to play on Opening Day," Moises
said.

When spring training started, Moises wasn't ready
to go full tilt with his teammates. He had only three or
four at-bats and didn't run because he could only run in a
straight line.

"I was afraid to make the turn. I had to get that out
of my head," said Moises, who had been hurt rounding first
base when he had come to a quick stop and his spikes caught
on the artificial turf at St. Louis.

On March 24, 1994, he was inserted into the outfield of a Grapefruit League game, his first game since in-
juring his ankle, and received a standing ovation from the
fans when he caught a fly ball.

Moises did make the Expos roster on Opening Day,
starting in left field for the second straight year. The first
two weeks of the season, he played every other day as he
continued to build up strength in his ankle.

"I couldn't play every day because I was in pain—plus we were playing on turf," he said of the opening series in Houston, then Montreal.

The Expos then traveled to the West Coast and softer grass fields, and Moises was able to play every day. He also was in pain every day. It hurt to take a step.

"Sometimes we think of it as a job and take things for granted," he said. "That day [when I fractured my ankle] made me really appreciate my uniform [and my] talent, and I think after that, I became a better ballplayer."

Moises had a tremendous year in 1994. He batted a career-high .339, third best in the National League, with 22 home runs and 78 RBIs. He ranked sixth in the National League in runs scored, hits, slugging percentage, extra-base hits, and total bases. He matched his career highs with four hits in a game and two home runs in a game three times each.

His comeback from ankle surgery was highlighted by his selection to the National League All-Star team in July. The game was played at Three Rivers Stadium in Pittsburgh, where Moises had made his major-league debut. It was a sweet coincidence, but one that his wife, Austria, had predicted.

After Moises had broken his ankle and was home recuperating in the Dominican Republic, he mentioned that he thought he may never play baseball again.

"My wife told me, 'You're going to be OK. You're going to be fine.' She said, 'Next year, you're going to be in the All-Star game," Moises said. "It sounded so far, like a fantasy."

But there he was, in the National League clubhouse with fellow All-Stars Barry Bonds, Tony Gwynn, Curt Schilling, and Jeff Bagwell.

"It was a thrill to be there," Moises said. "I had tears in my eyes. I thought about September 16 when I broke my leg and that seemed like yesterday and look where I am right now. That game had a special feeling."

Moises was not a starter. The National League team tied the game 7-7 in the ninth inning on Fred McGriff's two-run pinch homer off Lee Smith with one out. Moises was inserted into the game to play defense in the 10th inning.

In the bottom of the 10th, Gwynn, the batting star for the San Diego Padres, hit a bouncing single to center field. Moises was next, facing Chicago White Sox right-hander Jason Bere. Alou drilled the ball to the wall in left center. Albert Belle chased it down and fired to shortstop Cal Ripken Jr., whose relay to catcher Ivan Rodriguez was right there. But so was Gwynn, who had somehow wedged a foot between Rodriguez's shin guards at home plate, just ahead of the tag. The National League won, 8-7, to end the American League's six-year hold on the midsummer game. And Moises Alou, who thought his career was over, had the game-winning hit.

"It was a bang-bang play," Rodriguez said.

Moises had a tremendous year in 1994. Here he is shown delivering a hit that allowed Tony Gwynn to score the winning run in the tenth inning of the 65th All-Star gtame.

"The way guys were jumping up and down in here," David Justice said of the National League clubhouse, "you would've thought we'd won the World Series or something."

Clutch hitting was to become one of Moises' trademarks.

"He's a tremendous competitor, a fearless competitor," said Jerry Manuel, who watched Moises develop with the Expos.

The 1994 season was stellar not just for Moises but also for Montreal. The Expos exploded that year, boosted by such talent as Larry Walker, Pedro Martinez, Marquis Grissom, Sean Berry, and John Wetteland. Montreal finished the season with a 20-3 spurt and had a 74-40 record by August 11. The next day, the Major League Players Association went on strike. It was a major blow to the team and to manager Felipe Alou. Team owners canceled the remaining 249 games of the regular season plus all postseason play. The World Series, which had been played each year since 1905, did not occur.

The Expos claimed the mythical National League East title in the strike-shortened season, but the players will never know if they could have won it all. Felipe Alou was named Manager of the Year. It was bittersweet.

Moises was recognized for his standout season. He was named Latin American Player of the Year and finished third in the Most Valuable Player voting behind winner Jeff Bagwell of Houston and Matt Williams of San Francisco. Alou also was named Comeback Player of the Year.

Despite the Expos' success in 1994, Montreal's management started to dismantle the team. Montreal's small-market status hindered the team's ability to pay top salaries. Walker became a free agent. Wetteland was traded to the New York Yankees. Grissom was traded to Atlanta.

Labor discussions delayed the start of the 1995 season until late April.

Moises had more than baseball to deal with that year. On June 6, Moises made an off-balance throw during an Expos game at Los Angeles and tore his right bicep. On July 13, he damaged his left rotator cuff while diving for a ball against the Philadelphia Phillies. He aggravated the shoulder injury when he crashed into a wall at Philadelphia on August 14. Two days later, he pulled himself from the game in the first inning at New York.

Moises was placed on the disabled list and tried to recover from the injury. He returned for one game on September 9, making a pinch-hit appearance and drawing an intentional walk. That was all. He underwent arthroscopic surgery September 12 to repair the labrum in his right rotator cuff. On October 3, he had the same surgery to repair his left rotator cuff.

The injuries were much easier to deal with than the trauma the family faced on July 27. In Brooklyn, New York, two of Moises' in-laws were murdered in a shoot-out at a grocery store. Austria's father and brother were shot when a gunman tried to rob a store. Alou's father-in-law, Percio Melo, 54, had responded to the gunman by pulling his own pistol. Melo was shot several times in the upper body and died at the scene. Julio Melo, 32, Moises' brother-in-law, died about an hour later at a New York hospital.

Moises missed six games to attend the funerals and attempt to comfort his wife, who was pregnant at the time with their second child. When Austria gave birth on September 14, 1995, their son was named Percio in honor of her father.

The 1996 season gave Moises a chance to put his injuries behind him. He played in a career-high 143 games, establishing personal bests in at-bats (540), runs scored (87), and hits (152). He drove in 96 runs, the second highest season total by an Alou. His father Felipe had driven in 98 runs in 1962 for the San Francisco Giants.

Moises had started the year slowly, batting .262 prior to the All-Star break, but finished strong with a .319 average after July 25, including a .354 average in August. He collected three hits in back-to-back games twice—September 3 and 4 and September 17 and 18—and finished the year with 12 three-hit games and 38 multi-hit games.

Moises also added to the family scrapbook in the final game of the regular season. He was the last regular-season batter at Atlanta's Fulton County Stadium 30 years after his uncle Matty had become the first hitter in the ballpark's inaugural season. Felipe had been the Braves' lead-off batter in that very same game.

The Montreal Expos were 88-74 in 1996, the fourth-best record in the National League, and good for second place in the East division. It was an amazing accomplishment because the team had the lowest payroll in the major leagues. Together, Atlanta Braves pitcher Greg Maddux and Detroit Tigers first baseman Cecil Fielder made more than the combined 1996 salaries of the Expos—$15,737,500 versus $15,410,500.

The Expos roster had changed dramatically each year as players left the small-market club. "I knew I was the next guy to go," Moises said. "My dad knew it." They both understood the business of baseball.

CHAPTER 6
Florida and Houston

Father and son had a secret little whistle. Whenever Moises visits his father or his uncles in the Dominican Republic, he whistles as he walks to the front door. It is an Alou code. Felipe would use the whistle sometimes to get under Moises' skin.

"My dad, every at-bat, he wanted me to be so perfect on every pitch," Moises said. "If I took a bad swing, he'd yell, 'C'mon, Mo.' He knew the way I stand. Sometimes I get in trouble when I'm too wide and he'd whistle at me."

Don't think Moises was angry with Felipe. "My dad did that," he said, "because he cared about me."

It was time for Moises to see what he could do on his own. On December 12, 1996, he became a Florida Marlin.

Moises had become a free agent as part of baseball's new labor agreement. The Marlins offered a $25 million, five-year contract, part of the team's $89 million spending spree. Just four years in existence, the expansion Marlins had hired Jim Leyland as manager and committed the money to land six free agents: Alou, pitcher Alex Fernandez, infielder-outfielder Bobby Bonilla, outfielder Jim Eisenreich, pitcher Dennis Cook, and outfielder John Cangelosi.

During a spring training game in Viera, Florida, on March 14, 1997, Moises and his father were reunited, wearing different uniforms for the first time in five seasons. "There's a lot of things I'm going to miss over there," Moises said of the Expos. "Number one, I'm going to miss my dad. I had an opportunity to get to know him a lot better."

Moises' first at-bat at Miami's Pro Player Stadium in a Florida Marlins uniform was a memorable one. On April 1, in the second inning of the season opener against the Chicago Cubs, he lined a solo home run down the left-field line off Terry Mulholland. The Marlins went on to win 4-2. Moises was the third Marlins player to homer in his first at-bat. Mitch Lyden also did so June 16, 1993, and Terry Pendleton did on August 25, 1995. "He showed the fans why we signed him," Gary Sheffield said of Moises.

Funny thing is, Leyland had expressed some concern about Moises heading into the regular season. Alou had hit just .213 in spring training, the second-lowest batting average among the regulars. He also had been bothered by some nagging injuries—aches and pains involving his thumb, his shoulder, and his knee all slowed him in spring training.

On April 26 against Los Angeles, Alou seemed healthy, driving in all four runs in a 4-2 Marlins victory over the Dodgers. At that point, he was 10-for-21 with five home runs in his last six games and led the Marlins in every major hitting category, including average (.357), home runs (seven), and RBIs (22). He batted .360 with eight home runs and 30 RBIs in the first month of the season.

But in May, Moises went into a funk and batted just .247 with no homers and 13 RBIs. "I can look at videotape of what I'm doing differently or whatever," he said at the time. "But for me, it's right here." He pointed to his head.

Alou picked up the pace in June, hitting .293 for the month. He also became the player the Marlins wanted at the plate in clutch situations.

"He's a guy who wants to be up there if you're two runs down and have two guys on," said Marlins hitting coach Milt May. "The guys who are successful in those situations are guys who thrive on them and look forward to them. He was one."

You always knew when Alou was taking batting practice. All you had to do was listen.

"There are a few hitters in the league who have a little bit different sound," May said. "It's a little louder sound maybe. It's not always strength—that may be a part of it—but it's just a sound you get and you see that ball jump off his bat. It's something special and not a lot of guys have it, but he does."

Leyland heard it, too. "He's one of the stronger players in the league," Leyland said. "He's got a real still bat and hardly does anything with it and then *boom*. He's got tremendous bat speed. He's got tremendous strength from his elbow to his wrist. It's unbelievable."

Moises enjoyed playing outfield for the Florida Marlins. He felt that he fit right in and was very happy there.

Alou had an uncanny ability to come through in the clutch. "You look at the lineup and look at the innings and you think, 'If it's a crucial situation, let's hope Alou is the guy coming up to hit,'" Marlins broadcaster Joe Angel said.

Why did Moises do so well when it mattered the most?

"Because it's easier," he said after a game-winning, bases-loaded two-run single in the ninth inning on August 5 against Houston, and a bases-loaded, two-run single in the first against Pittsburgh the next day. "You only need to get a base hit with runners in scoring position. If nobody's on base, you try too hard to do something." Besides, he said, "hitting with nobody on base is boring."

Moises takes the old-school approach to hitting. He does not wear batting gloves. His stance is very upright and still. He cocks the bat over his right shoulder, poised to unleash his powerful stroke. The Miami fans looked forward to his at-bats and chanted "Alou, Alou" every time. "Mo was a popular player," Bonilla said. "Mo was the man there."

Moises fit the Marlins perfectly, and not just because of his baseball skills. His presence appealed to the

As seen in the photograph below, Moises takes an old-school approach to hitting. He does not wear batting gloves and his stance is very upright.

large Hispanic population in the Miami area. They could cheer for Alou or Bronx-born Puerto Rican Bonilla, Cuban-born Miami resident Fernandez, Colombian Edgar Renteria, or Jamaican-born White.

One day, the team was traveling on a bus and salsa music was blasting loudly from someone's portable stereo. No one seemed to mind. The Latin beat was pounding and lively. Moises surprised everyone by thanking them. "He was outwardly grateful for that moment," Angel said. "He said, 'I want to thank all of you, I really feel comfortable, I really feel great, this is an example of why it's great to be on this team.'"

The Marlins arrived in Chicago for a four-game series beginning August 25 right after the Expos had played there. Felipe had left his son a letter in the visiting clubhouse at Wrigley Field.

"It was probably the first letter my dad had sent me in 10 or 12 years," Moises said. "Every time he had sent me a letter and I opened the envelope, the first thing I did was to see if he sent me any money. When I opened this one, I checked, too—I'm not joking."

There was no money, but Felipe left a message that was even more valuable. "It was to congratulate me because he saw in the newspaper that I was doing very good," said Moises, who had showed the letter to everyone in the clubhouse. "When I signed with Florida, he wanted me to do good. When you get a multiyear deal like that, there's a lot of responsibility. He wanted me to look good in front of everybody."

Moises led the Marlins in runs (88), triples (5), home runs (23), runs batted in (115), total bases (265), and slugging percentage (.493). His RBI total was significant not just because it was best among the Marlins but because it was best among the Alous. Moises' 115 was a personal high and the best in his family, including those of his father and his uncles Jesus and Matty, whose records span 54 major-league seasons.

Bench coach Jerry Manuel was partly responsible for those RBIs. The coach had challenged Moises in spring training to drive in 110 runs. If he accomplished the feat, Moises said he would buy Manuel a new truck. As his RBI numbers kept increasing, Moises would stop by Manuel's locker and ask, "What color truck do you want?" He wasn't being cocky. Moises was confident he would come through.

At season's end, Manuel was driving a new truck, courtesy of Moises Alou.

In late September, Florida clinched the wild card spot in, of all places, Montreal. What a strange coincidence that Moises celebrated in front of his former team and his father. There was a play during the series when Moises ended up at third base after hitting a double and swiping the extra base on an error. He slid headfirst into third. "Those instincts run in our blood," said Felipe, who watched the play from the Expos dugout. "We don't allow our children to be afraid to perform. When you are afraid, you are cautious, and Alous can't be cautious on the baseball field."

The Marlins finished with the fourth-best record in the National League at 92-70 and won the wild card berth in the playoffs. Florida did reach the World Series, as detailed in Chapter 1, and won it all, beating the Cleveland Indians in seven games. After the victory, the players were cheered during a motorcade in downtown Miami. The celebration was short-lived. Marlins owner Wayne Huizenga had announced during the season that he was going to sell the team. The payroll had to be cut for the new ownership group, headed by Don Smiley.

Moises Alou was the first to go.

That November, the Marlins traded Alou to the Houston Astros for three minor-leaguers. The move was a $20.5 million slash of the budget over four years, which is what Moises was to have made through 2001. Alou was home in the Dominican Republic when he heard the news. His sister-in-law, Orquidia Melo, handled the flood of phone calls to his home in Santo Domingo. "He's not happy about it," Melo told reporters. "But he's OK with the new team."

Once again, Moises was a victim of the business of baseball. Florida general manager Dave Dombrowski called

A smiling Moises helped the Florida Marlins win the wild card spot in the playoffs and then go on to win the World Series in 1997.

Alou a "quality player and person" but said he had to separate himself from personal feelings in making roster moves. "It's not what you prefer to be doing, but we understand the situation," Dombrowski said. In building a World Series winner, Huizenga said he had lost more than $30 million. That meant that Dombrowski had to trim salaries to prevent another deficit for the new ownership. And that meant more departures.

After the Marlins dealt White and Robb Nen, Leyland called Moises. It was two weeks after Alou had been traded. He was still mad.

"I didn't have anything to do with it," Leyland told Moises, "and I was very upset about it, too."

"I was stunned," Bonilla said about his reaction when he heard that Moises had been traded.

"He was definitely a major player on the team, which is ironic because he was the first guy to go," Angel said.

Moises was shocked. "The game was improving after the strike, fans were coming back, and all of a sudden, they do that and it was a big step backward," he said. "We knew they were trying to sell the team, but nobody ever thought we'd break the team up."

It wasn't just that Moises had suddenly been separated from newfound friends. The 1997 Marlins never had a chance to defend the championship. That hurt.

"To win and then break the team up, that was the hardest part," Moises said. "When I got traded I was upset. I miss those guys. I miss being there. We had a special group."

CHAPTER 7
The Killer B's Add An "A"

The key players for the Houston Astros were Jeff Bagwell, Craig Biggio and Derek Bell. They were known as the "Killer B's." The Astros entered the 1998 season as the defending National League Central Division champions. That was Houston's first division title in 11 years. Bagwell, Bell and Biggio had combined for 80 home runs and 287 RBIs in 1997.

Moises Alou's name may not have fit but he was the perfect addition to the Astros. Inserted into the No. 5 spot in the lineup, Alou seemed right at home. He batted .341 in April and improved on those numbers in May. He won National League Player of the Week honors for May 25-31 when he hit .579 with two doubles, two triples, two home runs and drove in nine runs. His average peaked at .351 at the end of May and then he went into a little skid. On June 27, Alou delivered the go-ahead hit in the Astros interleague win over the Cleveland Indians with an RBI single in the 11th inning off Jose Mesa. "I haven't been playing the way I'd like to be playing lately," Alou said at the time, "but I knew (a slump) like this was coming, and I know how to get out of it."

He certainly did. The next day against the Indians, Alou homered, had three hits and drove in three runs to lead the Astros to a 12-3 romp over Cleveland. Alou didn't let up June 30 against the Chicago White Sox. He and Bagwell each hit two home runs and drove in four apiece to lead an 18-hit attack in a 17-2 Houston win. "It's nice to know if you're not hitting, someone else will pick you up,"

The Houston Astros were pleased to have Moises on board for the 1998 season.

said Alou, who recorded his first multihomer game of the season and the 11th of his career. The next night, Alou drove in four runs in Houston's 10-4 win over the White Sox. "I think this team makes me a better player, and I think I make this team better," Alou said. "This is probably the best I've ever felt this year."

Astros manager Larry Dierker was in his second season at the helm in 1998. He had pitched in the 1960s and had faced Moises' father Felipe Alou in games. Dierker noticed the similarities between father and son. "They're both very stoic, focused, quiet, no hot dog," Dierker said. "They respect the game and respect their teammates and opponents. They have the perfect attitude that you want a guy to have. Moises is very intense about winning."

Dierker also sensed that Moises knew what it meant to be an Alou. "It's like an obligation," Dierker said. "To me, it serves as a checkpoint. It's the way you're supposed to act and the things you're supposed to do and the mental toughness and the respect for the game and your teammates."

"Growing up as an Alou really helped me a lot," Moises said. "Why? Because I have to behave off the field.

I have to be a good citizen and I have to be a good player. I was a good player because I had the talent but I behaved good because of my father. My father is a well respected man in baseball in the United States and the Dominican Republic. Growing up, being an Alou, really helped me to be a better citizen and a better player."

The Astros led the Central Division at the all-star break. Alou was batting .314 with 20 home runs and 73 RBIs, and he was named to the National League All-Star team as a reserve. He was reunited at Denver's Coors Field with several former Florida teammates including Gary Sheffield (now with the Dodgers), Kevin Brown (San Diego), Robb Nen (San Francisco) and Edgar Renteria (Florida) as well as manager Jim Leyland. It was Alou's third All-Star game, and he went 1-for-3 but the American League beat his National League team, 13-8.

When regular season play resumed, Alou continued his offensive attack. On July 19, he hit his 23rd home run of the season, a three-run blast in the first inning off San Francisco starter Mark Gardner. The 23 homers matched Alou's career-high set in 1997 with Florida. He topped that on July 3 when he hit No. 24 in an 8-6, 10-inning win over Los Angeles. The two-run homer pulled the Astros within 6-4 and gave Alou his club-leading 84th RBI.

Playing for the Houston Astros was working out just fine. Alou constantly came through with big, clutch hits. He was not afraid of batting in any situation against anybody. On July 26, Alou faced San Diego's hard-throwing closer Trevor Hoffman in the ninth inning. The Padres led 4-3 and Hoffman was on a streak. He had tied the consecutive saves record of 41 the previous night. Alou ended it when he led off the ninth inning with a game-tying homer off Hoffman. "He was trying to get ahead of me," Alou said of Hoffman, who had struck Alou out the day before. "He did the same thing Saturday (July 25) and he got ahead of me with a fastball. This time, I was looking for it. I got it and I hit it."

When Hoffman enters the game, the public address system plays the loud sounds of AC/DC's "Hell's Bells." There was just silence after Alou connected for his 25th homer of the season. "That's the way the game of baseball

Alou connected for his 25th home run of the season.

is," Hoffman said. "You may be knocked one day, but you're going to be given the opportunity real quick to come back. [Alou] is the consummate professional and he did what he was supposed to with the pitch I gave him."

Alou homered in his next three games. "I've had this feeling many times but it's not a common feeling," Alou said after the Astros beat Florida 10-6 on July 30. "If it was common, I'd be in the Hall of Fame." He credited extra weight lifting as the reason he felt so strong.

The Astros added a strong arm on July 31 when they acquired left-handed power pitcher Randy Johnson from the Seattle Mariners in a blockbuster deal. "There are a lot of unhappy hitters in the National League right now," Alou said. Johnson led the American League in strikeouts with 213 at the time. Getting a big name player like Johnson boosted the Astros players' spirits.

"Nothing like this has ever happened here before, we've never picked up a guy of this caliber for the stretch run," Bagwell said. "That's why everyone is so excited. This is awesome." The Astros were leading the Central Division at the time of the trade but they also knew how important good pitching was. During last year's playoffs, the Astros were swept in the division series by pitching-rich Atlanta.

Alou just kept on hitting. Against the Chicago Cubs on August 15, he hit two homers, singled and scored three times in a 5-4, 11-inning come-from-behind win. It was Houston's 37th comeback victory of the season and just another typical Alou game. "I don't know if I have enough superlatives to talk about the kind of season he's having," Dierker said. Alou enjoyed the results. "Every time I go to the plate, I'm very confident," he said. "I like to be in the spotlight and in the pressure situations."

Alou's name was being mentioned as a candidate for the Most Valuable Player award, which is presented at the end of the season. "To me, he's the MVP in the league," said Astros reliever Jay Powell. "He does so much for this team. Moises always gets clutch hits, but this year it's just one after another. He's unbelievable." Biggio seconded the nomination. "He's got my vote right now," Biggio said.

If Dierker could vote, he said he'd cast a ballot for his left fielder. "I don't know how the voters vote," Dierker said of the balloting done by the Baseball Writers Association of America, "but my criteria would be the guy who means the most to his team, and Alou has been the most valuable. Without him, I don't know if this team would be where it is." The Astros were off to their best start in the franchise's history.

Houston had an impressive team. "I don't know how the Astros ever lose a game," Milwaukee manager Phil Garner said. "I'm serious about that. They don't make any mistakes. Their pitching has been superb."

And their hitting was incredible. For the first time in Astros history, four players had 20 or more home runs — and it was Alou and the Killer B's. Alou, Bagwell and Bell also each had at least 100 RBI.

Baseball became secondary in late September when Hurricane Georges ravaged Alou's homeland, the Dominican Republic. Alou's mother and oldest son, 6-year-old Moises Jr., were on the island when the storm hit, but neither was hurt. Their home in the capital of Santo Domingo was without power and sustained flood damage. Alou thought about home. Moises and his family live with his mother, Maria. He never wants to be too far from her cooking. Maria's specialty is red beans, rice and chicken.

There were still games to be played, however. The Astros clinched their second Central Division title and then reached another milestone. On September 23, Houston beat the St. Louis Cardinals 7-1 to win its 100th game of the season. The Astros became the third team in 1998 to reach 100 wins, joining the New York Yankees and Atlanta Braves. Since 1962, only 18 National League teams had won 100 games in a season. The closest Houston had come in years past was a 96-win season in 1986.

The Astros finished with a 102-60 record, second-best in the league to Atlanta's 106-56. Alou set career-highs in home runs (38), runs batted in (124) and games played (159). But his power numbers dropped off in the final month. It was not a good sign.

Even though father and son are now affiliated with different teams, they are very much in each other's thoughts.

The Astros led the National League in runs scored during the season and were counting on their high-powered offense backing Johnson in the playoffs. But Houston

struggled against West Division champion San Diego in the best-of-five Division Series. Padres ace pitcher Kevin Brown outdueled Johnson in Game 1, striking out 16 batters in a 2-1 San Diego win. The Astros edged the Padres 5-4 in Game 2 but that was the only bright spot. Brown started and won Game 3, 2-1, and Sterling Hitchcock pitched the Padres to a 6-1 victory in Game 4, again beating Johnson. The Killer B's were a combined 6-for-41 and Alou went 3-for-16 in the four games. "We got shut down," Johnson said. "Just shut down."

A pensive Alou is glad he extended his contract with the Houston Astros for the 1999 baseball season.

It was time to go home.

When the Astros played in Montreal in mid-May, Alou stopped by his father's office in the Expos clubhouse. Moises had a set of keys to a new car, a shiny black Mercedes Benz sedan. It was a gift from son to father.

"I have to give my dad credit," Moises said. "He came from a poor family, his dad was a carpenter. He struggled to go to school. I had a scholarship. I pretty much had everything. We struggled a little because he didn't make that much money but we always had food on the table and I always had an education."

Moises has one wish. He wants to play again with his father as manager. Father and son. Together, they will always have baseball.

MAJOR LEAGUE STATS

YR	CLUB	G	AB	R	H	2B	3B	HR	RBI	BB	AVG
1990	2TM	16	20	4	4	0	1	0	0	0	.200
	Pitt	2	5	0	1	0	0	0	0	0	.200
	Mon	14	15	4	3	0	1	0	0	0	.200
1992	Mon	115	341	53	96	28	2	9	56	25	.282
1993	Mon	136	482	70	138	29	6	18	85	38	.286
1994	Mon	107	422	81	143	31	5	22	78	42	.339
1995	Mon	93	344	48	94	22	0	14	58	29	.273
1996	Mon	143	540	87	152	28	2	21	96	49	.281
1997	Fla	150	538	88	157	29	5	23	115	70	.292
1998	Hou	159	584	104	182	34	5	38	124	84	.312
Totals		919	3271	535	966	201	26	145	612	337	.295

CHRONOLOGY

1966   Born July 3 in Atlanta, Georgia
1986   Selected by Pittsburgh in first round (second pick overall) in January free-agent draft; signed up May 23
1989   Married Austria on May 15
1990   Made major-league debut July 26, with Pittsburgh
Acquired by Montreal on August 16, 1990
1992   January 19 son Moises Felipe born
May 22, father Felipe named manager of Montreal Expos; Moises finished second in Rookie of the Year balloting
1994   Named to National League All-Star team and finished third in Most Valuable Player voting; named Latin American Player of the Year and Comeback Player of the Year
1995   September 14, son Percio born
1996   Granted free agency on December 5
Signed five-year, $25 million contract with the Florida Marlins on December 12
1997   October 9, son Kirby Thomas born
Led Marlins with 15 RBIs in postseason; Marlins won World Series 4-3 over Cleveland Indians.
Acquired by Houston on November 11, 1997
1998   Awarded Silver Slugger award as top outfielder, selected by managers and coaches

INDEX